# DYLAN'S DAY OUT

## Story and Paintings by
## PETER CATALANOTTO

Orchard Books · New York

Orchard Books, 95 Madison Avenue, New York, NY 10016
Manufactured in the United States of America. Book design by Mina Greenstein. The text of this book is set in 22 pt. Clarendon Book. The illustrations are watercolor paintings, reproduced in four-color halftone.
Hardcover   10   9   8   7   6   5   4
Paperback   10   9   8   7   6   5   4   3

Library of Congress Cataloging-in-Publication Data. Catalanotto, Peter. Dylan's day out / Peter Catalanotto.
p.   cm.   "A Richard Jackson book." Summary: Dylan, a dalmatian, escapes from his home and becomes involved in a soccer game between penguins and skunks.   ISBN 0-531-05829-8 (tr.)   ISBN 0-531-08429-9 (lib. bdg.)
ISBN 0-531-07034-4 (pbk.)   [1. Dalmatian dog—Fiction.   2. Dogs—Fiction.]   I. Title.   PZ7.C26878Dy   1989
[E]—dc19   88-36440

To JO-ANN...a rose with thorns

Day after day, Dylan's master went out.
There was no one to speak to.

Dylan could only stay, and sit...and dream.
Day after day.

But one morning, he found the door open.

This day was his...

...and off to the country he ran.

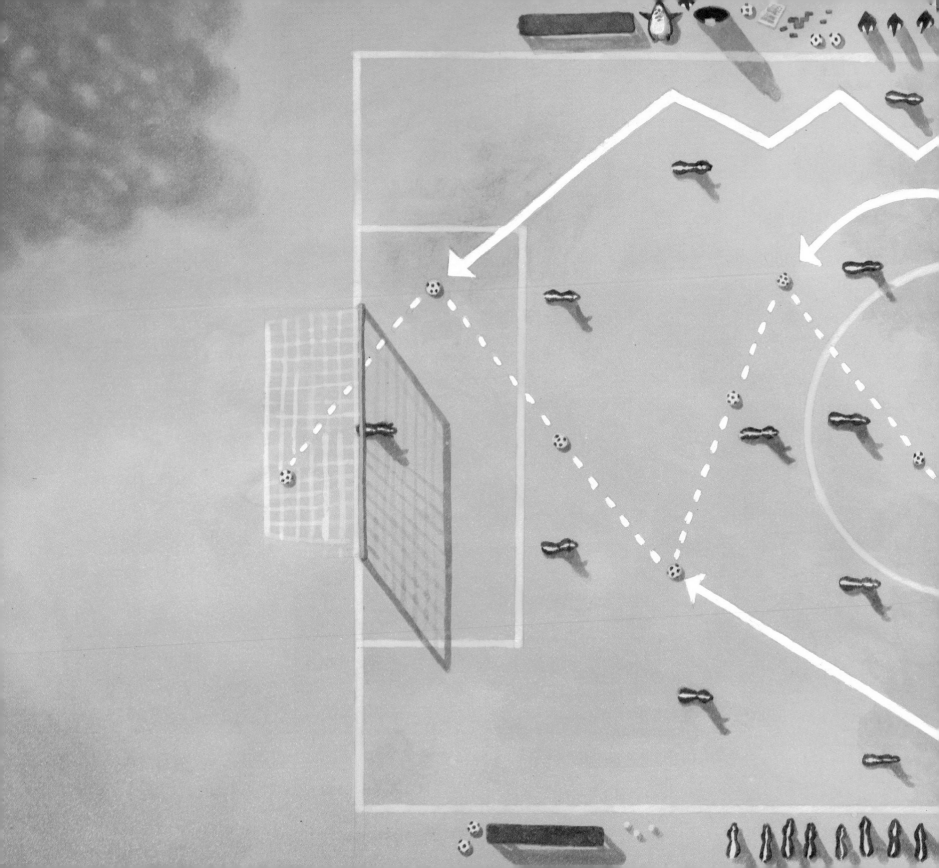

...So the game was won, the day was done

and Dylan...

...never said a word.